BLAKE
MORRISON

CAMP CUBA

PENGUIN BOOKS

PENGUIN BOOKS

Published by the Penguin Group. Penguin Books Ltd, 27 Wrights Lane, London
w8 5tz, England. Penguin Books USA Inc., 375 Hudson Street, New York,
New York 10014, USA. Penguin Books Australia Ltd, Ringwood, Victoria, Australia.
Penguin Books Canada Ltd, 10 Alcorn Avenue, Toronto, Ontario, Canada m4v 3b2.
Penguin Books (NZ) Ltd, 182 – 190 Wairau Road, Auckland 10, New Zealand · Penguin
Books Ltd, Registered Offices: Harmondsworth, Middlesex, England · These
extracts are from *And when did you last see your father?* by Blake Morrison, first
published by Granta Books 1993. Published in association with Penguin Books
1994. This edition published 1996 · Copyright © Blake Morrison 1993. All rights
reserved · The moral right of the author has been asserted · Typeset by Rowland
Phototypesetting Ltd, Bury St Edmunds, Suffolk. Printed in England by Clays
Ltd, St Ives plc · Except in the United States of America, this book is sold subject
to the condition that it shall not, by way of trade or otherwise, be lent, re-sold, hired
out, or otherwise circulated without the publisher's prior consent in any form of
binding or cover other than that in which it is published and without a similar
condition including this condition being imposed on the subsequent purchaser ·
10 9 8 7 6 5 4 3 2 1

I

A hot September Saturday in 1959, and we are stationary in Cheshire. Ahead of us, a queue of cars stretches out of sight around the corner. We haven't moved for ten minutes. Everyone has turned his engine off, and now my father does so too. In the sudden silence we can hear the distant whinge of what must be the first race of the afternoon, a ten-lap event for saloon cars. In an hour the drivers will be warming up for the main event, the Gold Cup – Graham Hill, Jack Brabham, Roy Salvadori, Stirling Moss.

My father does not like waiting in queues. He is used to patients waiting in queues to see him, but he is not used to waiting in queues himself.

A queue, to him, means a man being denied the right to be where he wants to be at a time of his own choosing, which is at the front, now. Ten minutes have passed. What is happening up ahead? What fathead has caused this snarl-up? Why are no cars coming the other way? Has there been an accident? Why are there no police to sort it out? Every two minutes or so my father gets out of the car, crosses to the opposite verge and tries to see if there is movement up ahead. There isn't. He gets back in and steams some more.

In the cars ahead and behind, people are laughing, eating sandwiches, drinking from beer bottles, enjoying the weather, settling into the familiar indignity of waiting-to-get-to-the-front. But my father is not like them. There are only two things on his mind: the invisible head of the queue and, not unrelated, the other half of the 2 country lane, tantalizingly empty.

'Just relax, Arthur,' my mother says. 'You're in and out of the car like a blue-tailed fly.'

But being told to relax only incenses him. 'What can it be?' he demands. 'Maybe there's been an accident. Maybe they're waiting for an ambulance.' We all know where this last speculation is leading, even before he says it. 'Maybe they need a doctor.'

'No, Arthur,' says my mother, as he opens the door again and stands on the wheel-arch to crane ahead.

'It must be an accident,' he announces. 'I think I should drive up and see.'

'No, Arthur. It's just the numbers waiting to get in. And surely there must be doctors on the circuit.'

He sits there for another twenty seconds, then leans forward, opens the glove compartment and pulls out a stethoscope, which he hooks over the mirror on the windscreen. It hangs there like a skeleton, the membrane at the top, the metal and rubber leads dangling bow-legged, the two ivory earpieces clopping bonily against each other. He starts the engine, releases the handbrake, reverses two feet, then pulls out into the opposite side of the road.

'No,' says my mother again, half-heartedly. It could be that he is about to do a three-point turn and go back. No it couldn't . . .

My father does not drive particularly quickly past the marooned cars ahead. No more than twenty miles an hour. Even so, it *feels* fast, and arrogant, and all the occupants turn and stare as they see us coming. Some appear to be angry. Some are shouting. 'Point to the stethoscope, pet,' he tells my mother, but she has slid down sideways in her passenger seat, out of sight, her bottom resting on the floor, from where she berates him.

'God Almighty, Arthur, why do you have to do this? Why can't you wait like everyone else? What if we meet something coming the other way?' Now my sister and I do the same, hide ourselves below the seat. Our father is on his own. He is not with us, this bullying, shaming undemocratic cheat. Or rather, we are not with him.

After an eternity of – what? – two minutes, we are up level with the cars at the head of the queue, which are waiting to turn left into the brown ticket holders' entrance, the plebs' entrance. A steward steps out of the gateway towards us, but my father, pretending not to see him, doesn't stop. He drives ahead, on to a clear piece of road where, two hundred yards away, half a dozen cars from the opposite direction are waiting to turn into another gateway. Unlike those we have left behind, these cars appear to be moving. 5

Magnanimous, my father waits until the last of them has turned in, then drives through the stone gateposts and over the bumpy grass to where an armbanded steward in a tweed jacket is waiting by the roped entrance.

'Good afternoon, sir. Red ticket holder?' The question does not come as a shock: we have all seen the signs, numerous and clamorous, saying RED TICKET HOLDERS' ENTRANCE. But my father is undeterred.

'These, you mean,' he says, and hands over his brown tickets.

'No, sir, I'm afraid these are brown tickets.'

'But there must be some mistake. I applied for red tickets. To be honest, I didn't even look.'

'I'm sorry, sir, but these are brown tickets, and brown's the next entrance, two hundred yards along. If you just swing round here, and . . .'

'I'm happy to pay the difference.'

'No, you see the rules say . . .'

'I know where the brown entrance is, I've just spent the last hour queueing for it by mistake. I drove up here because I thought I was red. I can't go back there now. The queue stretches for miles. And these children, you know, who'd been look-ing forward . . .'

By now half a dozen cars have gathered behind us. One of them parps. The steward is wavering.

'You say you applied for red.'

'Not only applied for, paid for, I'm a doctor, you see' – he points at the stethoscope – 'and I like being near the grandstand.'

This double *non sequitur* seems to clinch it.

'All right, sir, but next time please check the tickets. Ahead and to your right.'

This is the way it was with my father. Minor duplicities. Little fiddles. Money-saving, time-saving, privilege-attaining fragments of opportunism. The queue-jump, the backhander, the deal under the table. Parking where you shouldn't, drinking after hours, accepting the poached pheasant and the goods off the back of a lorry. 'They' were killjoys, after all – 'they' meaning the establishment to which, despite being a middle-class professional, a GP, he didn't belong; our job, as ordinary folk trying to get the most out of life, was to outwit them. Serious lawbreaking would have scared him, though he envied and often praised to us those who had pulled off ingenious crimes, like the Great Train Robbers or, before them, the men who intercepted a lorry carrying a large number of old banknotes to the incinerator ('Still in currency, you see, but not new so there was no record of the numbers and they couldn't be traced. Nobody got hurt, either. Brilliant, quite brilliant'). He was not himself up to being criminal in a big way, but he was lost if he couldn't cheat in a small way: so much of his pleasure derived from it. I grew up thinking it absolutely normal, that most Englishmen were like this. I still suspect that's the case.

My childhood was a web of little scams and triumphs. The time we stayed at a hotel situated near the fifth tee of a famous golf-course – Troon, was it? – and discovered that if we started at the fifth hole and finished at the fourth we could avoid the clubhouse and green fees. The private tennis clubs and yacht clubs and drinking clubs we got into (especially on Sundays in dry counties of Wales) by giving someone else's name: by the time the man on the door had failed to find it, my father would have read the names on the list upside-down – 'There, see, Wilson – no Wilson, I said, not Watson'; if all else failed, you could try slipping the chap a one-pound note. With his innocence, confidence and hail-fellow cheeriness, my father could usually talk his way into anything, and usually, when caught, out of anything.

He failed only once. We were on holiday, skiing, in Aviemore, and he treated us to a drink in one of the posher hotels. On his way back from the lavatories, he noticed a sauna room for residents near a small back entrance. For the rest of the week, we sneaked in to enjoy residents' saunas. On the last day, as we were towelling ourselves dry, an angry manager walked in. 'You're not residents are you?'

I waited for some artless reply – 'You mean the saunas aren't open to the public, like the bars? I thought . . .' – but for once my father stammered and looked guilty. We ended up paying some exorbitant sum *and* being banned from the hotel. I was indignant. I discovered he was fallible. I felt conned.

Oulton Park, half an hour later. We have met up with our cousins in the brown car park – they of course got here on time – and brought them back to the entrance to the paddock. My father has assumed that, with the red tickets he's wangled, we are entitled to enter the paddock for nothing, along with our guests. He is wrong. Tickets to the paddock cost a guinea. There are ten of us. We're talking serious money.

'We'll buy *one*, anyway,' my father is saying to the man in the ticket-booth, and he comes back with it, a small brown paper card, like a library ticket, with a piece of string attached to a hole at the top so you can thread it through your lapel. 'Let me just investigate,' he says, and dis-appears through the gate, the steward seeing the lapel-ticket and nodding him through: no stamp on the hand or name-check. In ten minutes or so my father is back. He whispers to my Uncle Ron, hands him the ticket and leads the rest of us to a wooden-slatted fence in a quiet corner of the car park. Soon Uncle Ron appears on the other side of the fence, in an equally quiet corner of the paddock, and passes the ticket through the slats. Cousin Richard takes the ticket this time and repeats the procedure. One by one we all troop round: Kela, Auntie Mary, Edward, Jane, Gillian, my mother, me. In five minutes, all ten of us are inside.

'Marvellous,' my father says. 'Three pounds eleven shillings and we've got four red tickets and ten of us in the paddock. That'd be costing anyone else twenty guineas. Not bad.'

We stand round Jack Brabham's Cooper, its
bonnet opened like a body on an operating table,

a mass of tubes and wires and gleamy bits of white and silver. Later, Moss overtakes Brabham on lap six, and stays there for the next sixty-nine laps. A car comes off the circuit between Lodge Corner and Deer Leap, just along from where we're standing. There is blood, splintered wood and broken glass. My father disappears – 'just to see if I can help.' He comes back strangely quiet, and whispers to my mother: 'Nothing I could do.'

2

She will sleep with him tonight. She worries that it's macabre, but I encourage her: she must do what feels right. And she says this is the last night she'll ever have him here, and she wants them to spend it together.

We are sitting on the bed round midnight, and

she is stroking his hand and kneading his face and then she tweaks his nose and says: 'Icy. But you never did complain of the cold, did you?' We have kept the window open, which is just as well because we've not been able to turn the radiator off and from time to time I catch a whiff of something I don't much want to think about. His face, the chin propped up on its T, is still perfect. He has always been a great sleeper ('I was really hard on,' he'd say when he woke from an afternoon nap or evening pre-pub zizz), and all this sleeping he is doing now seems his apotheosis – the hardest sleep of all. 'No, the easiest,' says my mother when I try this conceit on her: 'No dreams, no worries about oversleeping, nothing.'

She leaves the room and I lift back the sheet. It isn't him in quite the same savoury way now. There is a deep blackberry bruise spreading either side of the stomach scar – the skin looks papery-thin and in danger of oozing or bursting. Little red lines have appeared on parts of his bleached hands. The back of his neck, from what I can make out, has gone purple and discoloured, all the blood gathering there. I admire her for sleeping with him, but hope she won't slip between the same sheets, that she'll find a way to fold them so that her warm flesh isn't up against his cold.

When I come in at seven next morning, she's breathing beside him. Later, when I return, I find she's been crying.

'I've just been talking to my little man.'

'What about?'

'Oh, I've been telling him he shouldn't have gone and left me alone like this – not so soon.'

'I'm sure he didn't want to.'

'No, I know, I don't mean to be nowty. But the fact remains: he's upped and gone.'

She berates him some more, and I think of Cleopatra berating Antony:

> Hast thou no care of me, shall I abide
> In this dull world, which in thy absence is
> No better than a sty.

This is the way the world goes, the men running out on the women, running out *before* the women. A shorter life-expectancy: there's one great inequality men can brandish on their placards, can grumble about to women, who endure most of the others. But perhaps even in this women – as the ones left painfully behind while their husbands move beyond pain – end up suffering the most.

3

Sunday breakfast in the dining-room, the sun riding down from Embsay Moor. On the side-plates my father has laid out a series of vitamin pills: he has become fanatical about minding his As and Bs, his Cs and Ds, newly convinced that we can avoid colds and flu if we adopt a regime of tablets and capsules. Some of the pills are hard to swallow, others star-burst oilily when you nip their skin with your teeth. The family, not for the first time, is acting as a controlled medical experiment: what we are swallowing today, every patient in Earby will be swallowing tomorrow.

After toast and marmalade, my father and I retire to the two tip-back chairs which face out through the sash windows towards the moor. He is checking the share market, I the sports pages of the *Sunday Express*, where I stare for hours at the blurred anguish of a backward-arching goal-keeper. My mother, having cleared the breakfast stuff, is back again now with two mugs of coffee: 'Made with hot milk, Mummy? Smashing.'

It is my father who says this, not me. All through our childhood he has called his wife 'Mummy', never Agnes, her actual name, which he hates because it sounds drab and old-fashioned, never Kim either, the name her friends use and which he persuaded her to adopt not so much to seem chic and fifties – was it plagiarized from Kim Novak? – as to erase her rural Irish past. She has shed her name, abandoned her country and buried her Kerry accent; in return he calls her 'Mummy'.

'It's your half-term coming up,' he says.

'Hum.'

'I've been thinking. It's time we went camping.'

'Camping?'

'You know, fathead – tent, poles.'

'Hum.'

'Just the two of us, boys together – or *men* together.'

I have just had my twelfth birthday. This is what he must mean by 'men'. The thought of a camping holiday with my father fills me with dread.

'It's good to get away sometimes, you know – we love Mummy and Gillian, but there are things we're better off doing on our own, no faffing about or worrying if they're cold: you can't imagine them enjoying three nights in a tent like we will.'

'Hum.'

'Under the stars, fresh air and exercise – marvellous.'

A week later, on a hill above Lake Windermere, we're listening to the six o'clock news: there is something about Fidel Castro, with his big beard, and President Kennedy, who is so young and smily and perfect, and President Khrushchev, who my father says you can't trust. 'Secret installations', the newsreader says several times, and I think how difficult it must be to hide bombs: I have seen pictures of them and they are huge, or at least the clouds they give off are huge. Below, a rowing-boat chops and stitches its way across the water. The sheep on the green hills opposite are dotted tinily up to the summit, then evaporate into cumuli. 'Marvellous,' my father says. 'Couldn't have picked a better day. Fresh air, blue sky, not a soul in sight – makes you glad to be alive.'

I sit on the tartan rug while he reaches into the
boot, then dumps the heavy, rope-necked canvas

swagbag on to the turf beside me. He undoes the rope, then slides the bag along the length of tent and yanks it up, like a mother removing the dungarees from her flat-on-its-back, nappy-heavy toddler. It must be years since the tent was last up, on the beach at Abersoch or in the back garden, but at once a familiar smell rises from it – the smell of canvas and sand-dunes and grass cuttings and suntan oil and dead earwigs.

'Funny,' my father says, and goes back to the boot of the car. I get up, and fiddle with the guy-ropes, their heavy wooden adjustables.

'Is there a bag anywhere under the tent?' he shouts, as he opens the car door and peers under the back seat. I lift one corner and find a small blue canvas holdall.

'Yes,' I call.

'What's in it?'

'Pegs,' I shout back, pulling out a clunky handful of them – they look like primitive-man sticks of firewood, with little notches axed into the side.

'No poles?'

'No.'

I can remember what the poles are like – thick, wooden, three feet long, with large metal spears and slots at each end. I search the bracken, the canvas, under the car.

'I must have put them in,' my father says, without conviction.

'Couldn't we break some branches off and make do with those?'

'Don't be daft. It'll be dark in half an hour.'

'What are we going to do?'

'Pack up and go home.'

On the drove-road back down, though, he has another idea. 'We could stay in a hotel, I suppose.

And ring Mummy, and get her to drive up with the poles tomorrow and meet us halfway.'

Monday evening, with poles. After the misfortune of the night before – soon enough converted by my father into a huge joke against himself, the sort he could afford once he'd found the cosy hotel, with its log fire, consommé and roast duck – we have spent most of the day in the car. First we drove to meet my mother and sister in Kirkby Lonsdale, and had lunch. Then we came north again, nosing through the drizzle round Grasmere and Rydal Water, listening to the car radio, the weather forecast, the latest on Cuba. 'It's bound to clear up soon,' my father says, who is never one to complain, whose meteorology is a science of optimism. To him, rain is the natural order of things, which in the Yorkshire Dales is about right, and anything other than rain is a blessing. 23

'Lucky with the weather,' he'll say when it's heavy and overcast. 'Marvellous day' denotes high cloud. 'Miraculous, like being on the Riviera' is when the sun, however briefly, gets through the clouds.

At five we begin looking for a good pitching spot – 'I suppose there are official sites, but it's not the same as camping wild, and you have to pay.' We drive to Ambleside and Windermere: nothing. We take a left turn to Skelwith Bridge: the fields by the river are fenced off with barbed wire. We go back to Grasmere, through Chapel Stile, to the Dungeon Ghyll Hotel (trying not to notice the word Hotel), and as darkness begins to fall we settle on a spot by a stream. It is a low, unsheltered strip of flat grass. The farmer, though apparently surprised when we ask, has no objection to our being here. As my father's torch dims from a bright stare to yellow myopia – 'Bloody batteries gone already' – we get the last guy-rope secured, the last bendy leg of the camp-bed into its slot. It is only, what, seven-thirty, but I want to climb into my sleeping-bag.

We tie the tent flaps and set off for the pub, leaving the shaky house by the stream. As we drive, the Home Service is taken up with Presidents Kennedy and Khrushchev: the smily young hero has blockaded Cuba; Russian ships are sailing towards it. There are words I don't understand – diplomatic manoeuvres and retaliatory risks – and words that need no explanation, like World War Three. Will my father be too old to fight this time? I've had this daydream for years that if he's called up for war we'll keep him in the attic, like that picture I've seen at school of the Cavalier concealed in a tree-trunk. And if they send someone looking for him and ask me do I know where he is, when did I last see him, could they just look round, I'll not give him away, I'll keep his secret safe . . . Now the next war's nearly here, though, my plan seems childish. Maybe this time no one will have to fight, it can all just be push-buttons. We slam the car doors and step into the pub car park. Annihilation must look like the sky does now, blindness and blackness.

It's quiet inside, and the barman doesn't seem to notice my juniority (does he take me for fourteen? eighteen? is he pretending not to see?). The warmth and cigarette smoke and sawdusty floorboards create a fug of sociability, but it's hard to settle into, knowing we have to drive back to the cold tent, knowing the world may end. There are only men in here, big, smoking, laughing men jawing about war.

'Them bloody Russkies need a taste of their

own medicine,' says the fat one with sideboards

from his bar-stool. 'This Kennedy's called their tune. He's the first to stand up to 'em like we should have long since. I take my hat off to him.'

'Nay, Frank,' says the barman, 'the Reds an't been that bad. They've not dropped their bombs on anyone.'

'Maybe so, but they've got as far as Cuba, and this Castro bugger is standing there with open arms saying come on in, there's plenty room for thee, you can hide your nuclear weapons in my beard.'

'What a world it's coming to,' my father pipes up from our pock-marked brass table by the log fire, shaking his head, hoping some neutral, uncontentious remark like this will let him in on the conversation, will be the right kind of admission fee. The fat man with sideboards shuts up now, the barman goes off to serve another customer, and my father is left hanging there, at the edge of someone else's talk, wanting to insinuate himself, to be accepted. I know how it will go from here, because it's happened before in other pubs. My father will pick up our glasses, order another pint, start chatting to the man in sideboards, buy me shandy and crisps and say: 'Marvellous part of the world: wish I knew it better. What's your poison? Theakstons?' I am beginning to miss my mother. I don't want to watch what's going to happen happening: my father slowly winning over the suspicious locals; the conversation turning from world politics to legends of local brawlers, womanizers, con artists; the pint after pint, the whisky chasers, then the one for the road, and the next one for the road and the last one for the road. I stare at the smoke rising from the logs and imagine one wisp of it

journeying up the chimney and out through the

stack into the night, to dissolve in the immense black spaces and be gone from sight if anyone were looking, and yet not be gone, for surely nothing can be lost forever, every trace of whatever happened on the earth is recorded somewhere, even the dimmest or shortest life must have its immortality: the stars are shooting us for someone.

It seems very late, but perhaps it's no later than closing time when we leave, my father belatedly guilty at the sight of me sitting alone by the fire, a collage of deconstructed beer-mats across the brass table. The cold drizzle in the car park comes as a shock, and as we drive back the radio spits and crackles over the whish-whosh of the wipers – 'crisis', 'urgency', 'ultimatum'. Soon the headlights are picking out our frail little homestead: it looks like a story-book picture of the first pig's house, the one made of straw. The wind is getting up now, not to wolf-howl strength, but enough to growl and yank at the guy-ropes. We stoop inside, relieved to be out of the rain, but even my father's cheeriness can't make this a homely place, let alone home. He hands me a flask of coffee, with whisky added. 'That'll help you sleep,' he says, as my throat implodes, my stomach seethes with fission. I hear the rain beat the canvas. I hear the stream getting louder, more confident. I look up into the blackness and imagine Russian ships steaming across the dark sea and meeting American ships and all the bright final skies. There seems no kindly light that will lead us out of this, my father and me, here in our paper bag amid the encircling gloom.

We wake very early. The stream has burst its banks, and our tent, which has no groundsheet, is standing in an inch of water. Outside it's raining still and the wind whines to be off its leash. We drag ourselves out of our sleeping-bags and into our shoes, and splosh about in a sort of panic to be gone, breaking up the camp-beds, uprooting the pegs, dismantling the poles, tearing the canvas from its frame. It seems extraordinary, in the light of day, that we should have chosen this site – the stream looks higher than the fold of grass we pitched the tent in. But at least the tedious rituals of tent-packing can be dispensed with: we just dump the stuff higgledy-piggledy in the boot, and by eight o'clock are on the road.

It stops raining round four – 'Told you our luck was in' – but it's too late by then to think of drying the tent, even if the sun had come out, which it hasn't. There's nothing to stop us putting it up damp, of course, which is what my father seems determined to do. He gets the map out. 'Got it, just the spot,' he says, and we drive on through more flooded lanes, damp hedgerows, mist-obscured fells. 'Must ring surgery,' he says, pulling up by a red telephone box, not for the first time on this holiday, or others. Surely it's too early for surgery? Who can he be ringing? Through the mist of panes, I can see his head nodding. Any sane person would have called it quits by now, would have turned round and gone home, but here we are, proving ourselves hardy and hearty, pointlessly.

An hour later, I am sitting in front of a hotel lounge fire. My father fetches me a whisky mac: 'You're all right, they'll not notice, it'll help you thaw out. My feet are like ice.'

'Thanks, Dad.' He is still gloating at the trick he has pulled on me – trick or treat, I'm not sure which.

'Happier now?'

'Yes.'

'Maybe it's soft, but I didn't see any point sleeping in that sodding tent with the forecast for more rain.'

'You're right.'

'And it is our last night, and we're still boys away together. If I'd been on my own, or with Uncle Ron, I'd have stuck it, but there was no point making you miserable – I sometimes forget, you *are* only twelve.'

I let this go, too relieved to be here to argue. There is a television in the corner of the room, a little grey window high in a walnut tower, and when the news comes on there are pictures of a smiling President Kennedy: the Russian ships have turned back, the newsreader says, and Mr Khrushchev has agreed to dismantle all his missile bases in Cuba. A man with a microphone 33 stands in front of the White House and says: 'No one here yet knows what precisely made the Russians back down.'

My father and I clink glasses.

'Here's to Kennedy,' he says.

'To Kennedy,' I reply, my eyes watering over.

4

He is dead and I feel an odd triumph about it. He is dead, the thing (when I was small) I used to dread more than any other, but I'm still here, my mother's still here. I can hear her breathing, the world has ended but we've survived, we're OK. He is dead – no rage against the dying of the light, no terror and delirium, only a night-light smothered in its own wax. Sitting here, the body

silent between us as we peer into it for a sign of

some kind, I'm on a shock-induced high. If I listen hard enough, I know I'll hear his own count-your-blessings verdict: 'Well, that wasn't so bad, was it? When I think how it could have been – drawn-out, or abrupt and messy, or in hospital rather than here – it makes me feel lucky. A good death and a good life too: who could beat it?'

'The GP said to lay him flat.' My mother rises, icy calm, and we lift his head and remove some of the pillows from under it, straighten him on his back, pull his right leg up from its dangling position, and draw the covers up to his chest – why would anyone, except in the movies, draw them over the head, and shut out before time what will soon be unseeable forever? I'm crying quietly through this, and then leave my mother alone with him, and cry more noisily at the kitchen window. Outside is a tree-stump he left as a bird-table, with frills of white fungus growing out of its side.

I keep shooting back to see how she is, to see how he is. I feel a lifetime has passed, but the clock says seven-thirty, and here I am in the living-room, twenty, thirty minutes after his death, wading in boxes and boxes of photographs. It's something I do every Christmas, but Christmas has come a little early this year. Even now I can see it's some futile struggle to resuscitate and preserve him. His face swims up from the bendy sheens of black and white, the cardboard transparencies, the tiny sepia squares – in RAF uniform in the Azores; in his wedding suit in 1946; with a litter of twelve labrador pups, with babies, with toddlers, with his leg in plaster; being carried downstairs 'fresh' by a collection of male friends at his retirement party. There is something boyish and little in these that won't do, won't measure up. Then I find something better: a photograph of him outside our old rectory, leaning dandyishly against the side of his black Mercedes, a cigarette dangling from his right hand, his beautiful wife, fortyish then, posed beside him – an image of wealth and health and substance to set against the poverty and sickness we've lived with for the past month; an image, too, of the aspirations and affectations death has snuffed out.

There he lies, solid on his bed. I touch his skin. An hour after his death his forehead has cooled to marble already, but when I slip my hand under the covers and across his huge ribs, the chest is hot.

And it is still warm when the GP comes at nine: 'Poor Arthur, you didn't deserve this,' he says. And it is not much cooler – I know. I check – when Malcolm, the undertaker, arrives at eleven. He is fortyish, remembers me from school, is gangly in a grey suit with a Rotary Club badge on his left lapel: 'Oh dear, oh dear, Arthur,' he says and doesn't know where to put himself.

He asks for a bowl of water, and while my mother is out of the room uses a long tweezery implement to shove a piece of cotton wool into my father's open mouth, where it rests (visibly) at the back of the tongue – 'to stop any gases coming up,' he explains. My mother returns with the warm water. Malcolm takes a razor and for the next hour or so works away at my father's week-old stubble, 'just tidying him up.' I look at my mother and see that she is thinking what I am thinking – why bother with these cosmetics? Who will see him in the coffin? And even if he were to lie open for public viewing in a chapel of rest, who would mind the stubble? He might, I suppose: he was always a great one for checking whether I'd shaved. But he didn't like this sort of shaving himself – used only an electric razor – and would have resented the waste of manpower: better to have got Malcolm out doing something useful in the garden. If he'd been here, *really* been here, that's what he'd be arranging.

But my mother and I are new to all this, and yield to Malcolm's sense of etiquette. And at least it gives him something to do while he chats:

'I've done forty-eight this year – about one a week it works out. It's a sideline, the undertaking. My main business is joinery. But I don't get much call for that these days, and you've got to make ends meet. There's nothing special you want, is there? No? Fine. Of course some people want the works, you know, the whole waxworks. It's amazing what you can do these days – inject the client with formalin by sticking this tube into the neck artery, or drain the blood and urine off with an electric pump, and put caps under the eyelids to make the eyes more rounded, sleep and peace, like. I don't hold with that: making a corpse like a plum instead of a prune, it's not right. No embellishing, nothing fancy, simple and clean: that's my philosophy.'

I wait for the moment when he will nick my father's chin – do the unpumped dead bleed less profusely than the living? – but he does it all spotlessly. I help him roll my father on to his side, so he can remove the pads from under him, wash his bottom and put a fresh nappy between his legs: it's dirty work, but someone has to do it, and 'there may be more fluids,' he says. My father's body is a little stiffer now, but his back, as I hold him, is still warm, the skin red and corrugated where the sheet has wrinkled under him. 'This is why we come in fairly sharpish,' says Malcolm, 'before the rigor mortis. After

twelve hours they can be very stiff and hard to

move. After four or five days they go floppy again.'

My father said that he'd never wear a shroud in his coffin; and he would not have wanted to waste a good suit. So now I help dress him in a pair of fawn cotton pyjamas. Malcolm hasn't batted an eyelid yet, any more than my father has, but suddenly he seems flustered. I hold the body upright for him. He puts the right arm in the left sleeve, only realizing his mistake when he finds the pyjama buttons are underneath my father's back. We lift the body, and get the pyjamas off then on again the right way. They won't button up over the swollen stomach and zip scar, so we leave them open. There's one final cosmetic act: the chin support, a small white plastic T to keep the jaw from dropping too far open.

Once Malcolm has gone I sit with my father again and touch the little pacemaker box in his chest, sliding it about under the skin. My mother sits across from me, holding his hand. She has not cried properly yet: with each phone call – and as the day wears on there are more and more of these – her eyes water and her lips tremble, but she does not howl. Now, finally, she throws herself across him and sobs into his cold neck and chest.

5

When did you last see your father? Was it when they burnt the coffin? Put the lid on it? When he exhaled his last breath? When he last sat up and said something? When he last recognized me? When he last smiled? When he last did something for himself unaided? When he last felt healthy? When he last thought he might be healthy, before they brought the news? The weeks before he left us, or life left him, were a series of depletions; each day we thought 'he can't get less like himself than this,' and each day he did. I keep trying to find the last moment when he was still unmistakably there, in the fullness of his being, *him*.

When did you last see your father? I sit at my desk in the mortuary-cold basement of the new house, the one he helped me buy, his pacemaker in an alcove above my word processor, and the shelves of books have no more meaning than to remind me: these are the first shelves I ever put up without him. I try to write, but there is only one subject, him. I watch the news: Yugoslavia, the General Election, the royal separations – the news he didn't live to see. I've lost sight not only of his life, what it meant and added up to, but of mine. I feel as if an iron plate had come down

43

through the middle of me, as if I were locked inside the blackness of myself. I thought that to see my father dying might remove my fear of death, and so it did. I hadn't reckoned on its making death seem preferable to life.

When did you last see your father? A friend says: 'You know it's a painting, of course. Something to do with Charles the Second, I think. It hung on the stairs in my boarding-school, the first thing you'd see each term, just what you needed when your father had dumped you like a sack of potatoes. You know the one – it's incredibly famous.' I don't know it, or if I do I've forgotten. But suddenly everybody I meet seems to allude to it, or parody the phrase: variations on it are the stuff of sitcoms or Whitehall farce. I turn up the painting shortly afterwards, a Victorian tableau of the Civil War, the Cavalier boy stand-ing stiffly on a stool before a table of Puritan inquisitors – 'And When Did You Last See Your Father?'

I feel like an inquisitor myself. 'When did you last see *your* father?' I want to warn people: don't underestimate filial grief, don't think because you no longer live with your parents, have had a difficult relationship with them, are grown up and perhaps a parent yourself, don't think that will make it any easier when they die. I've become a death bore. I embarrass people at dinner parties with my morbidity. I used to think the world divided between those who have children and those who don't; now I think it divides between those who've lost a parent and those whose parents are still alive. Once I made people tell me their labour stories. Now I want to hear their death stories – the heart attacks, the car crashes, the cancers, the morgues.

The cursor pulses on the screen in front of

me. Some of my friends and contemporaries have written moving elegies for their fathers. Even when my father was in the best of health, I used to sit mooning and tearful over these poems as if they were for me, as if I'd written them myself. I wanted my father to hurry up and die so that I could join the club. I wrote an elegy for a friend of his, as preparation. I ran elegiac lines for him through my head. Now he's given me my opening, and the poems won't come.

Not that he'd mind much. He thought poetry all right in its way, so long as he didn't have to read it and I didn't suppose it a proper job. He said he couldn't understand my poems, and to me that was the ideal arrangement. I'd begun writing to escape him, to enter a world outside his control, so why would I have wanted him to get interested in my work? Perhaps the obscurity of some of my poems was there to keep him away

– just as, I now guiltily recognize, I put him off coming to the London newspaper offices I worked at and which he wanted to see ('It'd be nice to get an impression – how many people did you say you have under you? only two?'), and which he thought were regrettable but necessary steps towards the summit: a job in Leeds or Bradford ('just down the road from here – you could do it in fifty minutes') on the *Yorkshire Post*.

Only once, with the poetry, did I relent. It was 1985, and I'd won a prize, and invited him to the awards ceremony in County Hall. He turned up in his yellow-and-white Dormobile with stickers of the places he'd visited on the back window. It was loaded with wood he'd brought down from Yorkshire because my garden, he'd decided, was in need of some rustic fencing. In a big room overlooking the Thames, surrounded by poets, publishers, literary agents, people from the Arts

Council, he seemed small, shrunken, at a loss, a wine glass not a pint tankard in his hand. He wanted to enjoy himself, but he had a frowny, intimidated look about him, and I waited for him to make some withering remark about the company: 'Clever lot of buggers they think they are, eh?' Ken Livingstone was supposed to be there, and I knew my father had heard of *him*, but at the last minute Livingstone dropped out. Afterwards, someone asked my father what he thought of my poem, 'The Ballad of the Yorkshire Ripper', and he replied: 'The Yorkshire Ripper? Nothing very poetic about him.' He seemed to enjoy himself after that. We were supposed to go on to a meal somewhere, and he began trying to organize a large party, as if it were a midnight swim at Abersoch, everyone together, no shirkers, one big happy family. A large number of people were urged into the back of his Dormobile, between the rustic poles. I have suppressed the memory of who exactly he did give a lift to that night, but in my dreams Joseph Brodsky, Martin Amis, Craig Raine, Julian Barnes, Salman Rushdie and Dylan Thomas's daughter are driven over Westminster Bridge while my father explains that when you're putting up rustic fencing you must be sure to use six-inch zinc nails not four-inch iron.

Dreams? In truth, I don't dream of him. I dream of the vast ribcage of a bison lying on the sheet of the desert and being picked clean by vultures. I dream of blistered skin and crumbling parchment and a cyclone of paper bits, a lost masterpiece blowing about the sky. But I don't dream of him.

I tell the therapist this, as if it were a great discovery. Yes, Dad, a therapist. I know you don't approve, I know you're pretty down on analysts, 49 male or female (and this one's female), and yes *of course* I should have shopped around and found a cheaper one, or at least should have asked this one, instead of supinely writing the cheque: 'How much for cash?' But I do have to talk to someone; I'm not going to get through this alone. Not that we hit it off together all that well, she and I. There is no couch in her room, though there are beanbags, and a baseball bat to hit them with. Myself, I don't use the baseball bat, nor scream, nor weep. I sit in a white canvas chair, the sort film directors have, and I play her back bits of my life.

She catches me smiling at critical points of my psycho-story, and this, she says, or gets me to say, is because I'm trying to distance myself ironically from my emotions. She tells me I'm a poor communicator, that I don't listen to what my body's telling me, that I give out ambivalent signals. All of this is true, and helpful – so helpful that soon, I think, I shall stop seeing her.

In July I go up to Yorkshire – the first time in seven months. The village wants to remember you, Dad. You were going to be a bench at first, but there is a bench already, for someone else. Then you were going to be a tree, but they worried that in digging the hole they'd sever gas pipes or electric cables. So you have become a sundial instead. The wind blows through the delphiniums and the roses not yet deadheaded. The rustic fencing you put up rots at its own feet. The raspberries have mildew – they're grey and ashy like a dead mouse, and dissolve in the wind.

The ashes themselves, your ashes, have been kept in a big sheeny-brown plastic jar at the bottom of the wardrobe, and we've chosen today to scatter them. I take the jar down the garden, 51 unscrew the lid, dip my hand in and taste a few grey specks: a smoky nothingness on my tongue. You, or your coffin, or a crematorium pick 'n' mix, how can I tell? My mother and sister come, and we start to pour helpings of you among your favourite bits of the garden. We take it in turns, filling the lid of the jar with fine shale (like those upturned lids we used to fill with mouse poison and leave behind the fridge), then tossing the shale to the wind. The wind blows powder back in our faces; a speck catches in my sister's eye, her good eye; my trouser bottoms are sifted in volcanic dust. You cover the flower-bed like fine spray, every leaf variegated. We keep on scattering till the jar is tipped up for the last time. My mother hugs my sister. I walk off with the jar, which is like a giant pill-box, and hear your voice in the wind: 'Useful container that — I should hang on to it.' I stow it in the garage between the jump leads and a shrunken plastic bottle of anti-freeze.

Back in London, the therapist asks: 'How long did you say it had been now?'

'How long has what been?'

'Since the death. When did you last see your father?'

I remember the answer then. I tell her.

6

He isn't drinking, isn't eating. He wears his trousers open at the waist, held up not by a belt but by pain and swelling. He looks like death, but he is not dead, and won't be for another four weeks. He has driven down from Yorkshire to London. He has made it against the odds. He is still my father. He is still here.

'I've brought some plants for you.'

'Come and sit down first, Dad, you've been driving for hours.'

'No, best get them unloaded.'

It's like Birnam Wood coming to Dunsinane, black plastic bags and wooden boxes blooming in the back seat, the rear window, the boot: herbs, hypericum, escallonia, cotoneaster, ivies, potentillas. He directs me where to leave the different plants – which will need shade, which sun, which shelter. Like all my father's presents, they come with a pay-off – he will not leave until he has seen every one of them planted: 'I know you. And I don't want them drying up.'

We walk round the house, the expanse of rooms, so different from the old flat. 'It's wonderful to see you settled at last,' he says, and I resist telling him that I'm not settled, have never felt less settled in my life. I see his eyes taking in the little things to be done, the leaky taps, the cracked paint, the rotting window-frames.

'What's the schedule for tomorrow?' he asks, as always, and I'm irritated, as always, at his need to parcel out the weekend into a series of tasks, as if without a plan of action it wouldn't be worth his coming, not even to see his son or grand-children. 'I don't think I'll be much help to you,' he says, 'but I'll try.' By nine-thirty he is in bed and asleep.

I wake him next day at nine, unthinkably late, with a pint-mug of tea, unthinkably refused. After his breakfast of strawberry Complan he comes round the house with me, stooped and crouch-ing over his swollen stomach. For once it's me who is going to have to do the hammering and screwing.

I make sure there are only two light but time-consuming jobs for us. The first is to fix a curtain pole across the garden end of the kitchen, over the glazed door, and we spend the best part of two hours bickering about the best way to do this: there's a problem on the left-hand side because the kitchen cupboards finish close to the end wall, six inches or so, and you can't get an electric drill in easily to make the holes for the fixing bracket. The drill keeps sheering off, partly because I'm unnerved by him below, drawing something on the back of an envelope. I get down and he shows me his plan: a specially mounted shelf in the side wall to support the pole rather than a fixing bracket for it on the end. Sighing and cursing, I climb back up and follow his instructions in every detail – not just the size of screws and Rawlplugs needed, but how to clasp the hammer.

'Hold it at the end, you daft sod, not up near the top.'

56   'Christ, Dad, I'm forty-one years old.'

'And you still don't know how to hold a hammer properly.'

Infuriatingly, his plan works – the shelf mounting, the pole, the curtain, all fine. I try not to give him the satisfaction of admitting it.

We bicker our way into the next room and the other job: to hang the chandelier inherited from Uncle Bert. At some point in the move, many of the glass pieces have become separated, and now, in the dim November light behind the tall sash-window, we spend the afternoon working out where they belong, reattaching them to the wire that joins them. 'This really needs soldering,' he says, meaning that he will find an alternative to soldering them, since to solder would mean going out and spending money on a soldering iron when he has a perfectly good one at home. I watch him bowed over the glass diamonds, with pliers and fractured screw-threads and nuts and bits of wire 57

– the improviser, the amateur inventor – and I think of all the jobs he's done for me down the years, and how sooner or later I'll have to learn to do them for myself.

'I think that's it,' he says, attaching a last bauble. He stands at the foot of the stepladder holding the heavy chandelier while I connect the two electrical wires to the ceiling rose, tighten the rose-cover and slip the ring-attachment over the dangling hook. He lets go tentatively – 'Gently does it' – unable to believe, since he has not done the fixing himself, that the chandelier will hold. It holds. We turn the light on, and the six candle-bulbs shimmer through the cage of glass, the prison of prisms. 'Let there be light,' my father says, the only time I can ever remember him quoting anything, though I can recall some joke he used to tell, about failed floodlights at Turf Moor, a visiting Chinese football team, and the punch-line 'Many hands make light work'. We stand there gawping upwards for a moment, as if we had witnessed a miracle, or as if this were a grand ballroom, not a suburban dining-room, and the next dance, if we had the courage to take part in it, might be the beginning of a new life. Then he turns the switch off and it's dark again and he says: 'Excellent. What's the next job, then?'

PENGUIN 60s

READ MORE IN PENGUIN

For complete information about books available from Penguin and how to order them, please write to us at the appropriate address below. Please note that for copyright reasons the selection of books varies from country to country.

IN THE UNITED KINGDOM: Please write to *Dept. EP, Penguin Books Ltd, Bath Road, Harmondsworth, Middlesex UB7 0DA.*

IN THE UNITED STATES: Please write to *Consumer Sales, Penguin USA, P.O. Box 999, Dept. 17109, Bergenfield, New Jersey 07621-0120.* VISA and MasterCard holders call 1-800-253-6476 to order Penguin titles.

IN CANADA: Please write to *Penguin Books Canada Ltd, 10 Alcorn Avenue, Suite 300, Toronto, Ontario M4V 3B2.*

IN AUSTRALIA: Please write to *Penguin Books Australia Ltd, P.O. Box 257, Ringwood, Victoria 3134.*

IN NEW ZEALAND: Please write to *Penguin Books (NZ) Ltd, Private Bag 102902, North Shore Mail Centre, Auckland 10.*

IN INDIA: Please write to *Penguin Books India Pvt Ltd, 706 Eros Apartments, 56 Nehru Place, New Delhi 110 019.*

IN THE NETHERLANDS: Please write to *Penguin Books Netherlands bv, Postbus 3507, NL-1001 AH Amsterdam.*

IN GERMANY: Please write to *Penguin Books Deutschland GmbH, Metzlerstrasse 26, 60594 Frankfurt am Main.*

IN SPAIN: Please write to *Penguin Books S. A., Bravo Murillo 19, 1° B, 28015 Madrid.*

IN ITALY: Please write to *Penguin Italia s.r.l., Via Felice Casati 20, I-20124 Milano.*

IN FRANCE: Please write to *Penguin France S. A., 17 rue Lejeune, F-31000 Toulouse.*

IN JAPAN: Please write to *Penguin Books Japan, Ishikiribashi Building, 2-5-4, Suido, Bunkyo-ku, Tokyo 112.*

IN GREECE: Please write to *Penguin Hellas Ltd, Dimocritou 3, GR-106 71 Athens.*

IN SOUTH AFRICA: Please write to *Longman Penguin Southern Africa (Pty) Ltd, Private Bag X08, Bertsham 2013.*